MONSTER HEROES
THE HORRIBLE HEX

BY BLAKE HOENA
ILLUSTRATED BY DAVE BARDIN

STONE ARCH BOOKS
a capstone imprint

Monster Heroes is published by
Stone Arch Books, a Capstone Imprint
1710 Roe Crest Drive, North Mankato, Minnesota 56003
www.mycapstone.com

Library of Congress Cataloging-in-Publication Data
Title: The horrible hex / by Blake Hoena ; illustrated by Dave Bardin.
Description: North Mankato, Minnesota : Stone Arch Books,
a Capstone imprint, [2018] | Series: Monster heroes

Summary: Linda is a good witch, who always tries to undo the hexes that her
sisters, Agnes and Griselda, create—but to defeat the malevolent smoke that they
have cooked up this time, and teach her sisters a lesson, she will need the help of
her monster friends, Brian the zombie, Mina the vampire, and Will the ghost.

Identifiers: LCCN 2018013846 (print) | LCCN 2018016942 (ebook)
ISBN 9781496564214 (eBook PDF) | ISBN 9781496564139 (hardcover)
ISBN 9781496564177 (pbk.)

Subjects: LCSH: Witches—Juvenile fiction. Magic—Juvenile fiction.
Monsters—Juvenile fiction. | Sisters—Juvenile fiction. Heroes—Juvenile fiction.
Friendship—Juvenile fiction. | CYAC: Witches—Fiction. | Magic—Fiction.
Monsters—Fiction. Sisters—Fiction. Heroes—Fiction. Friendship—Fiction.

Classification: LCC PZ7.H67127 (ebook) | LCC PZ7.H67127 Ho 2018 (print) | DDC 813.6
[E] —dc23 LC record available at https://lccn.loc.gov/2018013846

Book design by: Ted Williams
Photo credit: Shutterstock: Kasha_malasha,
design element, popular business, design element

Printed and bound in the United States of America.
PA021

TABLE OF CONTENTS

MINA *(the Vampire)*

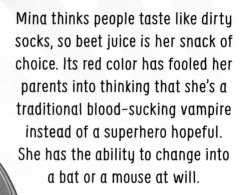

Mina thinks people taste like dirty socks, so beet juice is her snack of choice. Its red color has fooled her parents into thinking that she's a traditional blood-sucking vampire instead of a superhero hopeful. She has the ability to change into a bat or a mouse at will.

Brian is the brainy one amongst his friends. Unlike other zombies, Brian prefers tofu to brains. No matter what sort of trouble is brewing, Brian always comes up with a plan to save the day, like a true superhero.

BRIAN *(the Zombie)*

WILL (the Ghost)

Will is quite shy. Luckily he can turn invisible any time he wants because he is a ghost. When Will is doing good deeds, he likes to remain unseen. His invisibility helps him act brave like a real superhero.

With a wave of her wand and a poetic chant, Linda can reverse any magical curse. She hopes to use her magic to help people, just like a superhero would.

LINDA (the Witch)

CHAPTER 1

HEX POTION

KA-BOOM!

Linda jumped out of her seat.

"What was that?" she cried.

Peep. Peep! Petey squeaked.

Petey was Linda's pet. He helped her do witchy stuff. Only Linda understood what Petey peeped.

"I think you're right, Petey," Linda said. "My sisters, Agnes and Griselda, must be up to no good."

Peep. Peep! Petey squeaked again.

"Okay, let's find out what they're doing," Linda said.

Linda and Petey crept down the stairs one creaky step at a time. They peeked into the kitchen and gasped.

Linda's sisters were huddled around a black cauldron. So were their pets, Slither and Scratch. Smoke filled the room.

Agnes coughed. "Did it work?" she asked.

Griselda coughed too. "I don't know," she said.

Smoke poured out of the cauldron. Then it moved across the floor and under the door.

Slither hissed at the smoke.

Hiss! Hiss!

Scratch growled. *GRRR! GRRR!*

"It worked! The smoke has a
life of its own," Griselda screeched.

"Yes, let's see what it does,"
Agnes cackled.

Linda's sisters ran to a window. Linda did too.

The smoke wormed its way along the sidewalk. It snuck up behind a boy and grabbed his foot. The boy tripped, falling into a bush.

Then the smoke snuck up to a girl who was licking an ice-cream cone. It knocked the cone to the ground.

"It works! It works!" Agnes laughed.

"Our hex smoke will cause all sorts of problems!" Griselda laughed.

Peep! Peep! Petey squeaked.

"I know," Linda said. "We'd better get help."

CHAPTER 2

SECRET HIDEOUT

Linda waited for her friends at their hideout in the cemetery.

First Will floated through a window.

"Where's Brian?" he asked.

Then Mina flew in as a bat.

"Zombies are so slow," Mina said.

About an hour later, the trapdoor popped open. Brian crawled in.

Zombies were always late.

"So what's the problem?" Will asked.

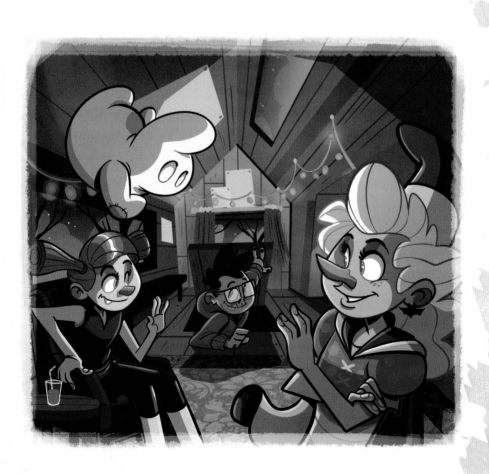

Linda told her friends what her sisters were doing.

"Your sisters created a cloud of smoke?" Mina asked.

"And it goes around hurting people?" Brian asked.

Linda nodded. "I know it's weird. But we need to stop it," she said.

Linda and her friends were not like other monsters. They did not want to scare people or hex them. They wanted to be like superheroes and help people.

"But how?" Mina asked.

"Easy," Brian said. "But first we need to find that hex cloud."

Linda and her friends left their hideout. They ran into town. What they saw there was frightening.

In the park, picnickers huddled under wet blankets. The hex cloud dumped rain on them.

At the basketball court, players could not make any baskets. The hex cloud kept knocking away the ball.

On the playground, the cloud pushed kids up the slide. It spun the merry-go-round too fast, and kids flew off. It lifted the swings out of reach.

"This is madness!" Will said.

Then Linda saw her sisters. They sat on a bench and watched what was happening. They laughed after every accident.

"Okay, it's time for our plan," Brian said.

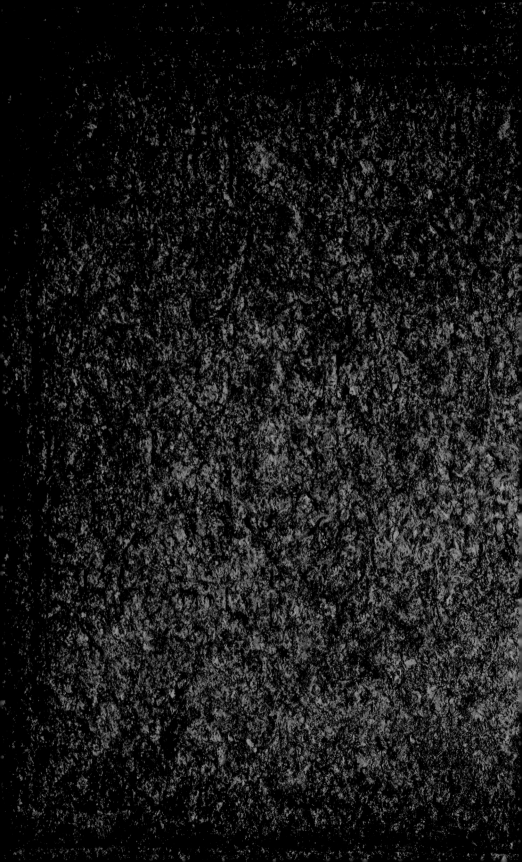

CHAPTER 3

WINGS AND WIND

POOF!

Mina changed into a bat.

Linda pulled out her wand.

She waved at Mina and chanted,

"Hocus-pocus turn humungous!"

Suddenly, Mina began to grow.

She grew from a little black bat

into a huge black bat.

"Now flap your wings," Brian said.

As Mina flapped, she created a gust of wind. The wind blew the smoke away from the picnickers. It pushed the smoke off the basketball court. It drove the smoke from the playground.

"Now blow the smoke at Agnes and Griselda," Brian said.

Mina blew the smoke toward Linda's sisters. Will helped direct it by waving his sheet. Linda helped by waving her wand.

The smoke was blown into the sisters. First it caused the bench they sat on to collapse. *THUD!* Agnes and Griselda fell to the ground.

Then it pulled their pointy hats over their heads.

"Hey, I can't see!" Griselda shouted.

"We need to get out of here!" Agnes cried.

Slither hissed and Scratch growled in agreement.

The sisters started to run off. Mina continued to blow the smoke after them.

It grabbed their feet, and they fell into a bush.

It lifted Scratch and Slither into the air. The witches grabbed their pets to keep them from flying away.

The sisters ran into the house and huddled around the cauldron. They made another spell to reverse the smoke.

Thankfully it worked right away. Linda and her friends laughed.

"That will teach them to make such mean hexes," Linda said.

"It sure will!" Mina said.

Agnes and Griselda just moaned from the kitchen.

BLAKE HOENA

Blake Hoena grew up in central Wisconsin, where he wrote stories about robots conquering the moon and trolls lumbering around the woods behind his parents' house. He now lives in Minnesota and continues to write about fun things like space aliens and superheroes. Blake has written more than fifty chapter books and graphic novels for children.

DAVE BARDIN

Dave Bardin studied illustration at Cal State Fullerton while working as an art teacher. As an artist, Dave has worked on many different projects for television, books, comics, and animation. In his spare time Dave enjoys watching documentaries, listening to podcasts, traveling, and spending time with friends and family. He works out of Los Angeles, California.

GLOSSARY

cauldron—a large kettle, often associated with witches' brews

cemetery—a place where dead people are buried

chant—to say or sing a phrase over and over

hex—a magical spell that is meant to cause bad luck for someone

hideout—a place where someone hides to avoid being found or captured

reverse—to turn something around

TALK ABOUT IT

1. Linda and her friends don't want to cause trouble. They want "to be like superheroes and help people." If you could be a superhero, what would your superpower be? Would you use it to help people?

2. The Monster Heroes have a secret hideout in the cemetery. If you could have a secret hideout, where would it be? What would it look like?

3. If you were Linda, what would you say to your sisters? Would you try to explain what they did was wrong?

WRITE ABOUT IT

1. Use your imagination and write the recipe for a potion. Be sure to write out how much of each ingredient the potion needs and name it.

2. The group solves their problem by turning Mina into a giant bat whose wings can control the smoke. What are other ways they could have stopped the sisters' smoke from getting out of control?

3. Would you rather be a witch, a vampire, a zombie, or a ghost? Write a paragraph explaining your answer.